For Michele

*Faith, hope, and love
are the best gifts of all*

Before Christmas, decorating day is special to our family because our tree gets decorated with memories!

THE ORNAMENT HOSPITAL

WRITTEN BY Andy Williams

ILLUSTRATED BY Tami Boyce

ISBN: 9798678881878

Printed in the United States of America

Almost all our ornaments remind us of past trips and fun times together, or places where we've lived. As we pull each one out, we laugh and smile about the good times we've had.

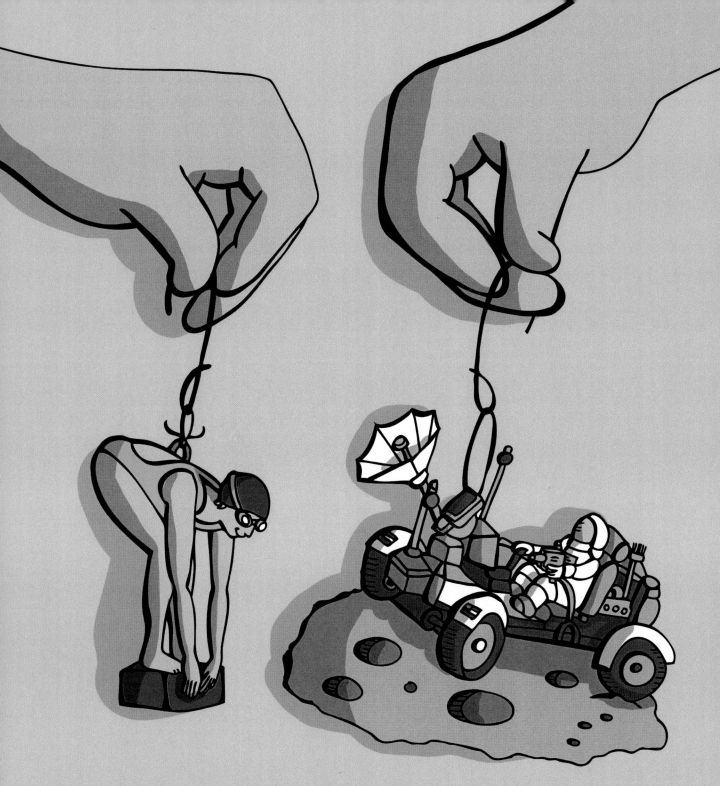

We have a swimmer for our daughter who loves the water, and a NASA lunar rover for our son who dreams of walking on the moon.

Mom loves remembering when the children were younger, so she enjoys the handmade ornaments created by the little children's hands.

And me? I like riding my bicycle,
so I have an ornament of Santa
riding a bike!

All ornaments are different—some just hop right out of their boxes every year, and they're ready to go on display. Some ornaments aren't ready to create memories, so they take their special place filling in the empty spaces on the tree. And the ornaments that make the best memories? They take their place right where everyone can see them!

Unfortunately, accidents can happen, and sometimes an ornament does not make it out of the box in one piece. A part falls off here, a string breaks, or an angel's wing pops off. It's sad for all the ornaments and our family to see a broken memory.

To keep all the ornaments in working order so they can create memories and make people smile, we have faith in the magic of Christmas.

At Christmas time, my workbench becomes The Ornament Hospital, where the ornament magic happens!

Years ago, one of our daughter's favorite ornaments had a little accident in the box and wasn't going to make it to the tree. As our son unpacked the decorations box, that favorite ornament got set aside to be forgotten.

Not wanting his sister to be sad at Christmas, he hid the ornament, and said that if she believed in the magic of the Ornament Hospital, it might come back for a visit.

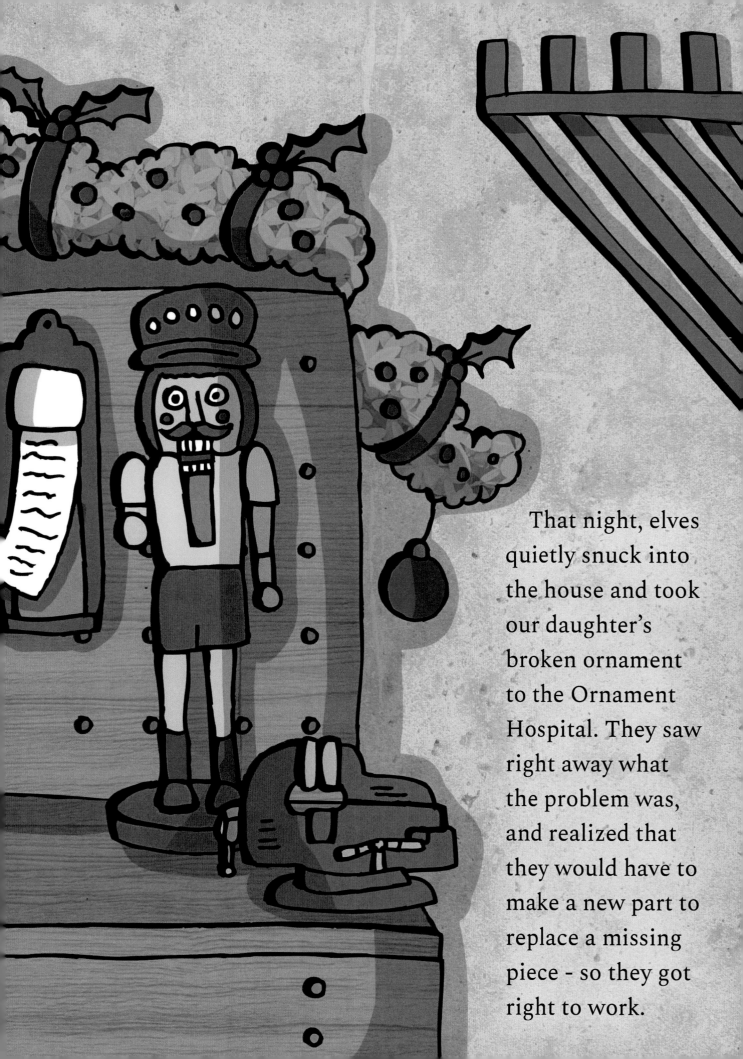

That night, elves quietly snuck into the house and took our daughter's broken ornament to the Ornament Hospital. They saw right away what the problem was, and realized that they would have to make a new part to replace a missing piece - so they got right to work.

It took hours to fix the broken ornament.
And wouldn't you know it? With a nutcracker keeping
an eye on the work, the paint and glue dried in no time; and
the newly fixed ornament was rushed out of the Ornament
Hospital and to the tree before the sun came up!

The other ornaments started cheering and clapping as
they welcomed their friend back. It was a wonderful time
for all the decorations!

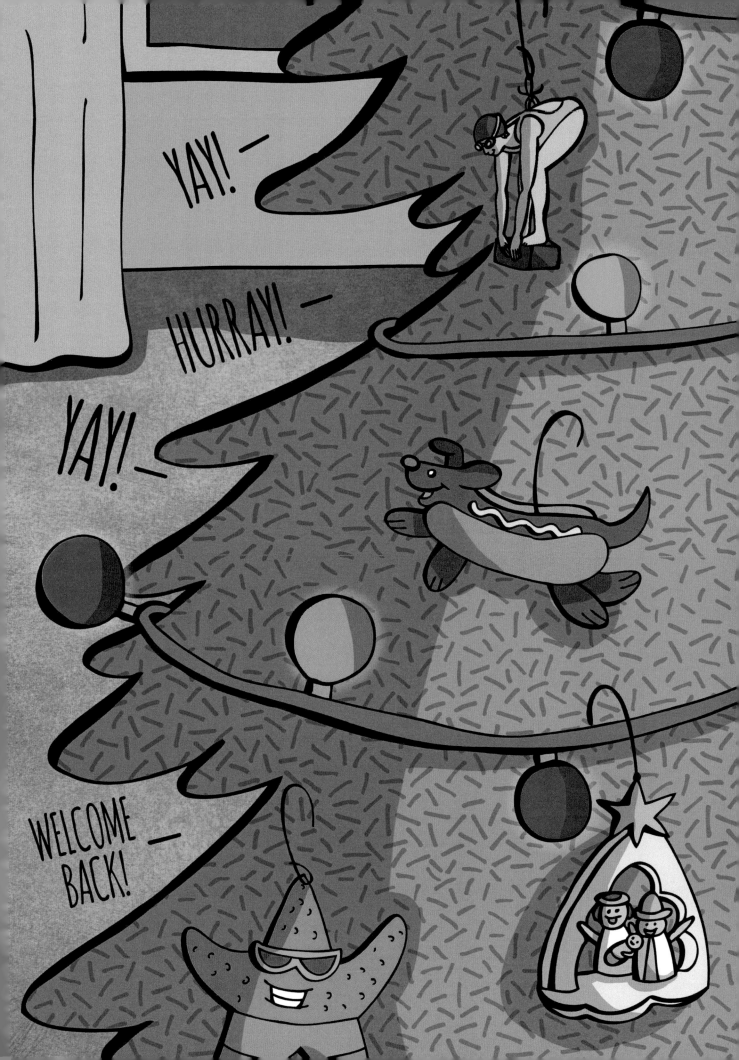

The next morning, I was reading the paper, and Mom was making breakfast when our kids came downstairs. "Hey!" our son said to his sister. "Look at the tree!!"

The Christmas magic had done it again!

The End

About the Author

ANDY WILLIAMS lives in McKinney, Texas (and no, he doesn't sing) along with his wife Michele, and Rocky the cat who is well-known for carefully guarding the neighborhood. Originally from Charlotte, North Carolina, Andy has two grown kids with their own families and friends in Colorado and Tennessee. When not helping companies find great employees, Andy can be found riding one of his bicycles, playing vinyl records, or hanging out with the guys in his church's men's group. He loves writing silly short stories and since he's quite accident-prone on those bicycles, writing at his desk is probably the safest place for him! The "real" ornament hospital has traveled with him over the years and sits in his garage.

About the Illustrator

TAMI BOYCE, an illustrator and graphic designer with a fun and whimsical style, is based in Charleston, South Carolina.

"Holding a pencil in my hand has been my passion for as long as I can remember. I count myself as an extremely lucky individual because I have been able to make a career out of it. We all live in a very serious world, and I like to use my quirky style to remind us of the love, joy, and humor that is often overlooked around us."

To see more of Tami's work, visit tamiboyce.com.

Made in the USA
Las Vegas, NV
30 March 2021

THE ORNAMENT HOSPITAL

is a children's lesson about caring for others, set around the scenes that many will recognize from their own recollections of the Christmas holidays. It's a gentle reminder that tending to the little things brings joy and happiness; and shares the secrets of faith, hope, and love through its tale of broken and redeemed ornaments brought back to life. You'll enjoy reading this children's Christmas classic with family and friends, and will want to revisit it year after year.

ISBN 979-8-6788-8187-8

9 798678 881878

90000>

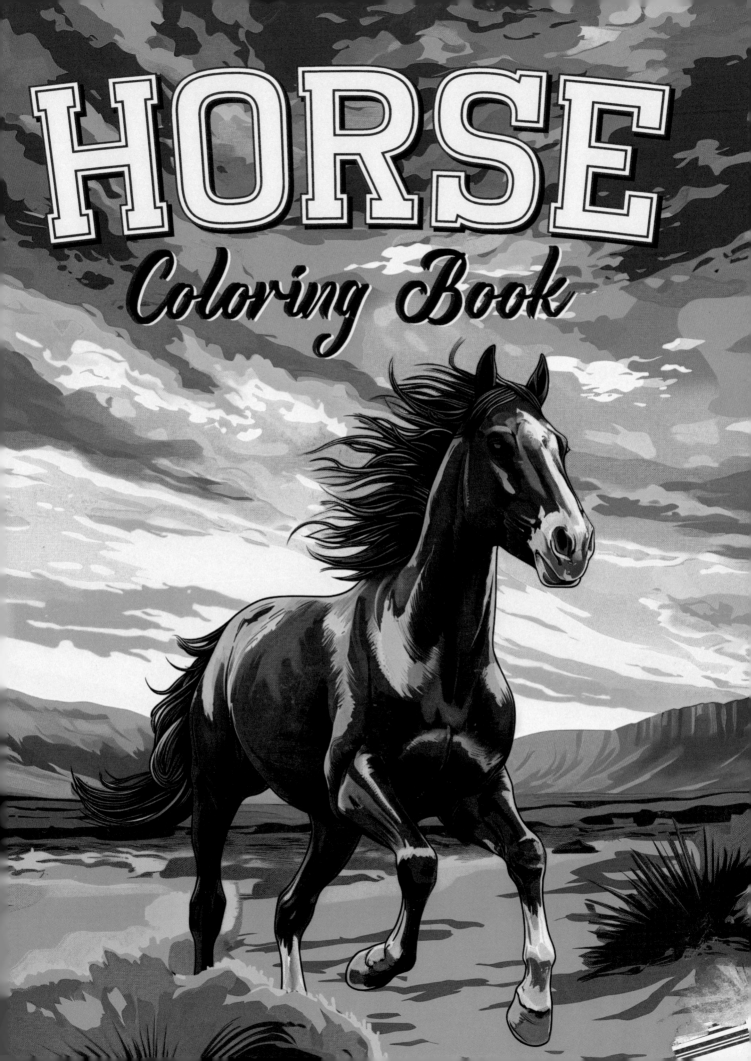